To: Decker

We love You! Can't wait to meet you!

♡ you lots,
The Cordivari's

This igloo book belongs to:

.....Decker.....Reed.....................................

igloobooks

Illustrated by Sanja Rescek
Written by Melanie Joyce

Cover designed by Lee Italiano
Interiors designed by Justine Ablett
Edited by Hannah Cather

Copyright © 2016 Igloo Books Ltd

An imprint of Bonnier Publishing USA
251 Park Avenue South, New York, New York 10010
Manufactured in China. DIS002 0118
10 9 8 7 6 5 4 3 2

Library of Congress Cataloging-in-Publication
Data is available upon request.

ISBN 978-1-78670-188-6
IglooBooks.com
bonnierpublishingusa.com

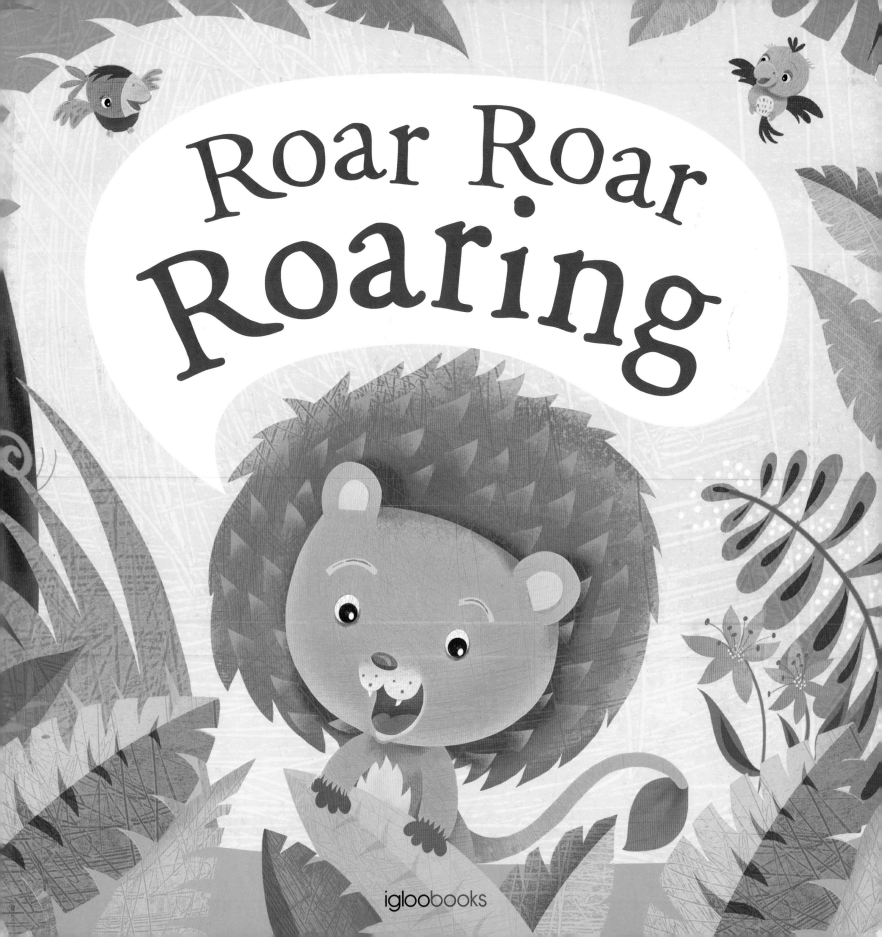

Roar Roar Roaring

igloobooks

Roar goes Lion and shakes his shaggy mane.
Squawk go the parrots. Squawk, they go again.

It's a roar-snore-Squawk noisy jungle day.

The monkeys all start swing-swing-swinging, oo-oo-ooing as the birds are singing.

ROAR!

Tweet-tweet-tweet go the birds all around.
Oo-oo go the monkeys, swinging to the ground.

It's a **swing-oo-oo-tweet** noisy jungle day.

The zebra chews the grass and it's **yum-yum-yummy.**
He **chomp-chew-chomps** and fills up his tummy.

It's a **clomp-stomp-chomp** noisy jungle day.

The hippo in the mud is
gloop-gloop-glooping...

... sinking slowly, bloop-bloop-blooping

The **swishy** little fish all **wiggle** their fins.
They all **splash** out, then **sploosh** back in.

ROAR!

It's a gloop-bloop-**splash** noisy jungle day.

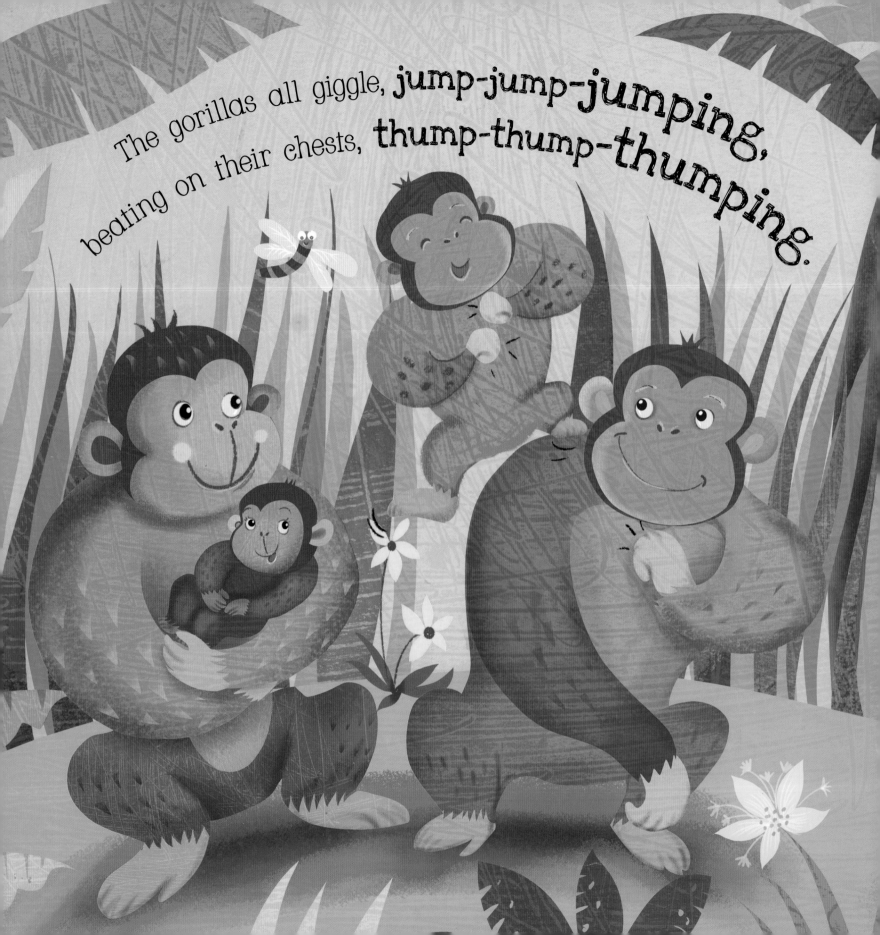

The gorillas all giggle, jump-jump-jumping,
beating on their chests, thump-thump-thumping.

A toothy crocodile is creep-creep-Creeping past the leopard, who is sleep-sleep-Sleeping.

ROAR!

SNAP goes the crocodile.
SNAP, SNAP, SNAP.

He wakes up the leopard from his cozy nap.

It's a creep-sleep-snap noisy jungle day.

The little elephants are **play-play-playing.**
Their curly trunks are **sway-sway-swaying.**

The cheetahs run by, chase-chase-chasing, all around the jungle, race-race-racing.

The giraffe is happy to munch-munch-munch, nibbling at the high leaves, crunch-crunch-crunch.

It's a **chase-race-crunch** noisy jungle day.

Soon the sun is glow-glow-glowing,
above the river that's flow-flow-flowing.

Everyone is tired after all that play.
They've had such a lovely jungle day.

It's a **glow-glow-flow** noisy jungle day.

Lion and the parrot stop **roaring** and **squawking**.
There's no more **swinging** or **stomping** or **clomping**.
No more **glooping, blooping,** or **jumping**.

No more creeping, sleeping, playing, thumping, swaying, chasing, racing, munching, crunching.

Sleep-sleep-Snore is the only jungle sound.